Hannah's Temper

Celia Berridge

Cartwheel B·O·O·K·S™

Scholastic Inc.

New York   Toronto   London   Auckland   Sydney

Originally published in 1992 in the U.K. by André Deutsch Children's Books/Scholastic
Publications Ltd.

Text copyright © 1992 by Celia Berridge.
Illustrations copyright © 1992 by Celia Berridge.
All rights reserved. Published in the U.S.A. by Scholastic Inc.,
730 Broadway, New York, NY 10003, by arrangement with
Scholastic Publications Ltd.
CARTWHEEL BOOKS is a trademark of Scholastic Inc.

Library of Congress Cataloging-in-Publication Data

Berridge, Celia.
    Hannah's temper/Celia Berridge.
      p. cm.
    Summary: As one thing after another goes wrong for her, a toddler becomes increasingly bad-
tempered.
    ISBN 0-590-45887-6
    [1. Behavior — Fiction. 2. Mother and child — Fiction. 3. Stories in rhyme.] I. Title.
PZ8.3.B459Han 1992
[E] — dc20   92-10874
                                                                                                 CIP
                                                                                                  AC

12 11 10 9 8 7 6 5 4 3 2 1   3 4 5 6 7 8/9

Printed in Malaysia

First Scholastic printing, May 1993

Hannah's in a temper;
Hannah's in a stew.
She's making quite a fuss
And a huge hullabaloo.
Mama says, "What's all that noise?
Why don't you go and play?"
But everything is going wrong —
Oh, what a grumpy day!

Hannah's in a temper;
Hannah's in a state.
She goes outside to play and snags
Her sweater on the gate.
Hannah gives a mighty tug —
The sweater rips its hood!
Hannah smacks that naughty gate
And shouts, and kicks the wood.

Hannah's in a temper;
Hannah's in a rage.
She goes to play with Bunny but
He nips her through his cage.
She only put her finger
Just a small bit through the door,
But Bunny didn't like it, and
Now Hannah's hand is sore.

Hannah's in a temper;
She's really in a spin.
She slammed the door so hard before
That now she can't get in.
Hannah knocks and bangs and yells,
But Mama isn't near.
She's in the kitchen mixing dough
So loud, she just can't hear.

Hannah's in a temper;
There's nothing she won't do!
She pulled apart the cat door
And stuck her head right through.
Mama comes and says, "You goose!
Keep still; don't squirm about."
But Hannah cries and wriggles 'round
Until her head is out.

Hannah's in a temper;
She's feeling very mean.
She scribbles all along the wall
That Mama just washed clean.

She scribbles underneath the coats;
She scribbles by the stair.
Mama stops her just in time.
And sits her in her chair.

Hannah's in a temper;
Hannah's in a huff.
She wants some more banana;
She hasn't had enough.
Mama says, "You've had a lot;
You won't eat any more."
So Hannah takes her dinner plate
And throws it on the floor.

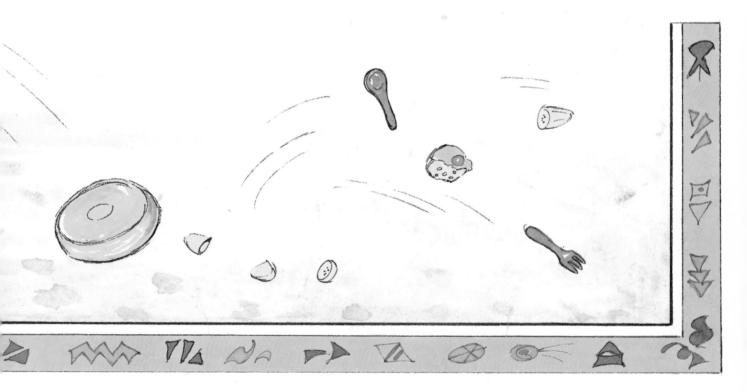

Hannah's in a temper —
Hear her puff and shout.
She stuffed her teddy down her boot
And now he won't come out.
Hannah pulls and twists and tugs,
Then bangs the boot so hard
That teddy shoots out of the boot
And lands in the backyard.

Hannah's in a temper —
Hear her shout and scream.
She takes off all her clothes and then
She squirts the shaving cream.
Mama says, "Hop in the shower;
You look like cotton candy!"
But Hannah wants to stay that way —
She thinks the mess is dandy.

Hannah's in a temper;
She makes an awful mess.
She sprinkles powder on the chairs
And on her clean green dress.
Mama says, "Oh, Hannah, no!
What's wrong with you today?"
But Hannah shouts and stamps her foot
And tries to run away.

Now Mama's in a temper;
Now Mama's in a huff.
Hannah's been a naughty girl
And Mama's had enough.
Mama says, "You're going to bed;
The best place for a pest.
Maybe you'll feel better when
You've had a little rest. "

Hannah's feeling better now,
But just a wee bit sad.
She's sorry for those naughty things
That made her Mama mad.

Mama says, "Did you feel sick?
Was that what bothered you?"
Then Hannah laughs — and Mama says,
"Oh, look! Your tooth's come through!"